The Wild West
Goes Crazy

BILL CONDON

Illustrated by Geoff Hocking

Triple3Play

Published by
Sundance Publishing
P.O. Box 1326
234 Taylor Street
Littleton, MA 01460
800-343-8204

First published 2001 as Supa Dazzlers by
Pearson Education Australia Pty Limited
95 Coventry Street
South Melbourne 3205 Australia
Exclusive United States Distribution: Sundance Publishing

ISBN 0-7608-6180-3

Printed in Canada

Contents

For Marion Smith, a great teacher, and for the children she taught at Willala School

Chapter 1

Ready
for
Action

"Where do you want to go now?" asked Dad. "Ancient Egypt? Old Rome? Just say the word and we'll be off, Kendra. The time machine is ready for action!"

Kendra thought it over. Ancient Egypt would be cool. When she grew up, she wanted to be a doctor, so she was very interested in bandages. And mummies have a whole lot of bandages. Old Rome would be OK, too, since Kendra loved pizza.

It was hard to choose. Then Kendra thought about how much Dad loved watching westerns on TV.

He'd sit alone in the living room, munching popcorn and wearing a cowboy hat. Every now and then he'd yell "Yippee!" at the TV. It was almost as if he expected it to yell "Yippee!" back. It was all very strange, but Dad was like that sometimes.

"I've made up my mind," she said. "I'd like to go back in time to a place where only the tough survived."

"You mean kindergarten?" Dad asked.

"No! I want to go to places like Tombstone and Dodge City. Back to the days of the Wild West!" said Kendra.

"You mean cowboys and cowgirls?"

"Yes, Dad. And even cows! Can we go there?"

Dad's eyes sparkled. "Wild horses couldn't stop us, Kendra. Let's saddle up the time machine."

Chapter 2

Vulture Gulch

From the outside, the time machine looked only big enough to hold two people. But Dad had added walls and ceilings that expanded. Plus there were two extra floors that opened with the flick of a switch.

Now the time machine had much more than a lab. It had a toilet that flushed when the user whistled. It also contained a small swimming pool and the very newest computer games. Dad also had added a video library with the best movies and an old-fashioned bowling alley.

Dad was still adding things when Kendra spoke up. She said, "I think that we have enough stuff."

Dad stopped working for a moment. "So you don't want the roller coaster?"

"No, Dad."

"What about the race-car track?"

"No, Dad."

"OK," he said with a shrug. "I guess we'll have to rough it."

Dad set the dial on the time machine to land in the town of Vulture Gulch in 1880.

"My research shows that Vulture Gulch was one of the scariest towns in the West," Dad said. "We'll be lucky to get out of this in one piece! I'm so happy!"

"On second thought, maybe we shouldn't visit a really scary place," Kendra said nervously. "Can't we just visit some place that's only mildly scary—like a Wild West goat farm?"

"Don't worry," Dad said. "The worst that can happen is we'll get captured by bandits. Or the time machine will blow up."

"I've changed my mind, Dad. I don't want to go anymore," said a worried Kendra.

"Too late! Buckle up, Kendra. We're off to the Wild West!"

Chapter 3

The Hall of Shame

The time machine made roaring sounds like a fire-breathing dragon that had an awful toothache.

Then it rattled and spun as if it was out of control. It felt like it was about to break into a thousand pieces. And it kept spinning faster and faster.

Gripping her chair tightly, Kendra yelled, "Dad! I'm scared!"

"So am I, Kendra," laughed Dad. "So am I! But isn't this great fun! I'm having such a blast!"

WHOOSHHHHH!

There were booms and crashes, followed by dead silence.

It was pitch black. It was bright light.

They were climbing. They were falling.

And then the time machine bounced six times and landed gently.

Dad opened the hatch and jumped out. Kendra was right behind him.

"That's Vulture Gulch ahead of us," said Dad. "Let's go explore."

Soon they were standing in the middle of a dirt road. It had wooden shops on both sides. All around them were people riding horses. They wore western clothes (the people, not the horses), just like they wore in the movies.

A sign above one of the buildings said:

WILD WEST HALL OF SHAME

Three cowboys stood in front of the building.
They all had bushy beards and tubby
tummies. And they were crying their eyes out.

"What's wrong?" Kendra asked.

"We've just won an award," they sobbed.

Dad looked surprised. "An award? But surely that's good, isn't it?"

"No! It's terrible! We've been voted the top three failures in the Wild West. We're the stars of the Hall of Shame!"

Chapter 4

Three Cool Cowboys

The cowboys seemed more than a little odd. One hiccuped every second word. Another had loud rumbling noises coming from his stomach every few seconds. The third cowboy was a mighty burper. His burps were louder than a herd of burping buffalo!

"We'll help you," promised Dad.

"No one can help us," said the burpy cowboy.

"You're wrong," replied Kendra. "We're inventors."

"From the future," Dad added.

The burper and the rumbler almost fainted in shock, but the hiccuper was all smiles. "I had a feeling we'd meet someone like you today," he said. "Welcome!"

The cowboys introduced themselves as Wild Bill Hiccup, the Lone Rumbler, and Quiet Burp.

"Of course, those aren't our real names," said Quiet. "But they're the names everyone calls us. Actually they call me Booming Burp, but I prefer Quiet."

Dad and Kendra listened closely as the trio told their story. They had all been partners in a fast-food cafe called The Big Cactus.

The Big Cactus
Specials

Cactus Burgers and Beans

Cactus Hot Dogs and Beans

Cactus Fries and Beans

Cactus Pizza and Beans

Cactus Coffee and Beans

"Do you still own the cafe?" asked Kendra.

"Shucks, no," said the Lone Rumbler. "That cafe is history."

"For some reason," explained Wild Bill, "folks just didn't take to eating cactus and beans."

"We worked our fingers to the bone at The Big Cactus for a whole year," recalled Rumbler. "But no one came in."

"Of course, we couldn't waste good food," added Quiet. "So every day for a year we ate all of the cactus and beans ourselves."

Quiet's eyes filled with tears.

"Now all of that fast food has turned us into the loudest and silliest cowboys who ever rode the range," he sobbed.

Chapter 5

Three Sad Stories

"I'm very sorry," said Kendra.

"That's nothing!" replied Wild Bill. "Wait until you hear what happened next."

Dad's eyes were wide. "Oh, please tell us."

"Well," Wild Bill went on, "after we closed the cafe, I wanted to be a famous sheriff."

"I wanted to be a champion rodeo rider," said Rumbler.

"I wanted to be a singing cowboy," said Quiet.

"All fine career choices," nodded Kendra.

"You're right, little lady! But things didn't go as we hoped," Quiet told her.

"I was about to have a shooting match with Fast Draw Bob Bore," said Wild Bill. "But I let loose with such a mighty hiccup that my suspenders snapped. Down went my pants!"

"I was riding in a rodeo when my stomach let out a loud rumble," said the Lone Rumbler. "It scared my horse so much that it fainted. And all of the other horses ran away!"

Finally, Quiet told his sad story.

"I was treated by Dr. Belcher, the famous burp expert. He told me that I was cured," Quiet said. "So I entered the Skunk Hill Singing Cowboy Contest. I was singing a song when this lady in the front row started munching cactus-and-bean ice cream. I just snapped! The burps jumped out of me like mad bullfrogs. The people ran for their lives."

Suddenly Quiet threw himself at Dad's feet.

"Help me!" he cried.

The Lone Rumbler and Wild Bill looked sadly at Dad and Kendra.

"Tell us the truth," said Wild Bill. "Can you help us?"

"Sure we can," said Kendra. "Right, Dad?"

"No problem!" he replied.

Chapter 6

Rumbler Rides Off

Dad and Kendra quickly came up with a plan. While Dad worked in the lab, Kendra showed the trio western movies on TV. She thought it would be good if they watched movie heroes like Slopalong Cassidy. They'd learn lots of cowboy tricks.

But the plan backfired. Slopalong got into a shooting match on the show. When that happened, Rumbler, Wild Bill, and Quiet fired their six-shooters at the TV! **KABOOM!**

The TV screen exploded into little pieces, and smoke flowed through the time machine.

"That will teach those outlaws," said Quiet.

Dad rushed into the room. "Is everything all right?"

"Yes," said Kendra. "But I don't think that they're big fans of western movies."

Dad was too happy to care about the explosion for very long. He'd just finished his latest invention, and he wanted to show it off.

Outside the time machine, the cowboys watched Dad. He placed a large piece of rubber on the grass. "This is for you, Rumbler," he said.

"Wow!" replied Rumbler. "Thank you! I don't know what to say. This is awesome! I'm so happy! What an honor!"

"Do you know what it is?" asked Dad.

"I have no idea," replied Rumbler.

"It's a horse!" Dad said.

"It sure doesn't look like a horse."

"It's a special kind of horse," explained Dad. "When you push this button on its neck, it fills up with air. And this horse isn't afraid of *any* noises. Not even the loudest rumbles!"

With a grin, Rumbler sat on the piece of rubber and pushed the button. The rubber grew and took shape. In under ten seconds, Rumbler was riding tall in the saddle.

"Yippie!" Rumbler yelled. "Now I'll be king of the rodeo!"

As he galloped around, the horse grew bigger and bigger.

"You'd better stop pushing that button!" warned Kendra.

"No sirrr-ee!" shouted Rumbler. "I'm having too much fun!"

Soon the rubber horse was as large as a midsize dinosaur. Then it lifted into the air and floated away!

"Ye-haaaaaa," called Rumbler, as he disappeared into the sunset.

"Oops," said Dad.

Chapter 7

The Burp Bouncer

Dad and Kendra felt awful about Rumbler, but Wild Bill put their minds at ease.

"I'm sure he'll come down in a few years," Wild Bill said.

"Besides," added Quiet, "I've never seen old Rumbler so happy."

Dad left it to Kendra to come up with the next invention. Within an hour, she wheeled out something that looked like a huge dish.

"It's a Burp Bouncer," she said proudly. "I'll put it in front of Quiet when he sings."

Kendra went on, "The sound of your burps will bounce off the dish and leap right out into the audience. That way it will seem as if *they're* burping instead of you, Quiet! It's a perfect plan!"

Quiet clapped his hands with delight. "Hot dog, little lady!" he hooted. "That sure is a doozy! Let's try it!"

Once again Quiet entered the Skunk Hill Singing Cowboy Contest. He was halfway through his song when a fierce attack of the burps hit him.

Kendra switched on the Burp Bouncer. Just as she'd promised, Quiet's huge burps bounced into the audience.

Suddenly people stopped listening to Quiet and started looking around. They began pointing at their neighbors and accusing them of burping rudely.

"It wasn't me," said the mayor standing up quickly.

"Oh, yes it was," said his wife.

"I didn't do it!" protested a little girl. "It was my big brother!"

"Was not!" howled the brother.

More and more people were getting upset. The crowd turned over tables, threw pies, and yelled at each other.

The judge of the singing contest, Annie Jokely, was not amused. "This is all your fault!" she told Quiet. "I'll make sure you never burp in this town again!"

Chapter 8

The Hiccuping Cowboy

Just when it looked like things were getting really bad, a well-dressed lady came up to Quiet.

"I heard what that woman said to you," she told Quiet. "Is it true? I have to know for certain! Are you the one responsible for all of those burps?"

"I'm afraid so," Quiet replied.

He expected that she'd be angry with him. But instead she threw her arms around Quiet and kissed him.

"What was that for?" asked Quiet.

"Please excuse me," she begged. "But I've traveled all over the world looking for someone exactly like you. And now I've found you!"

"I don't understand. Why have you been looking for someone like me?" asked Quiet.

"Allow me to introduce myself," she said. "I am Lady Belle Ringer, of the Belle Ringer Opera Company."

"You don't say!" said Quiet.

"Ah, but I do say," replied Lady Belle. "And I want you to be the star of my newest opera—*The Burping Prince*."

"Yes!" cried Quiet. "I'm your man!"

With that, Quiet and Lady Belle held hands and walked away.

While Dad thought of new inventions, Kendra searched the Internet. As well as hiccup cures for people, she found hiccup cures for dogs, cats, and mice. She even found a cure for hiccuping hippos!

All of the cures said one thing. The only way to get rid of hiccups was with a fearsome fright!

Chapter 9

A Shocking Cure

Of course, Dad and Kendra couldn't tell Wild Bill about the cure. It wouldn't work if it wasn't a surprise.

"Just go into town and wait," Dad told him.

"Wait for what?" Wild Bill asked.

"You'll see," Kendra said, winking at Dad.

The next day, a horse-driven wagon arrived in town. In the wagon was a huge black box. The driver looked exactly like Dad, except that he had a hairy red beard. He jumped off the wagon.

Then, as the driver ran away, he yelled, "It's a bomb!"

A couple of brave cowboys tiptoed close to the box. They could hear a loud ticking noise coming from inside it. They also found a note that said:

Lift the lid—if you dare.

The townsfolk went to the mayor. They asked him what he planned to do about the bomb.

"I plan to go on vacation!" he said. "See you in six months."

Everyone was afraid, even the great bomb expert Rex Plode. "Ticking bombs are the worst kind," he said grimly. "Only a very silly person would attempt to lift the lid on that box."

Wild Bill stepped forward. "I guess that means me," he said. "I'll do it . . . if you make me sheriff."

The townsfolk roared their approval. They pinned a sheriff's badge on Wild Bill before he could change his mind.

Wild Bill had never been so happy in his life. But he'd never been so scared, either.

Wild Bill's hands shook so much that his fingers were in danger of falling off.

His legs trembled so hard that his feet jumped right out of his boots.

He almost drowned in the puddle from his sweat.

And then he started to hiccup!

The whole town put their hands over their ears and waited for the bomb to go off!

Chapter 10

The Hall of Fame

Ever so slowly and with a great deal of care, Wild Bill lifted the lid a tiny bit. He closed his eyes and held his breath. He waited, but nothing happened.

Working up all of the courage that he could gather, he lifted the lid a little more. Still nothing happened.

By now the suspense really was beginning to get to him.

Between hiccups, he shouted "I can't stand it anymore!" And with one mighty pull, he lifted the lid off the box.

Something jumped out at him! It leaped and at the same moment screamed, "**BOOOOO!**"

Just as loudly, Wild Bill screamed, "**I WANT MY MOMMY!**"

He was ready to run all of the way back home. Then he realized that it wasn't anything bad. It was only Kendra.

"Sorry to trick you," she said. "But you needed a good scare to get rid of your hiccups . . . and it worked!"

"You'll never have the hiccups again," laughed Dad, coming out of the crowd. He was holding his fake red beard.

"Yippee!" cried Wild Bill. "This is the greatest day of my life. No more hic-hic-hic-hic . . ."

"Oops!" said Dad, as Wild Bill hiccuped louder and longer than ever before.

But luckily, the hiccups no longer mattered.

"Wild Bill is still the bravest man in town, hiccups or no hiccups," said Annie Jokely. "He'll always be our sheriff!"

Soon it was time for Dad and Kendra to say good-bye. They had one last meeting with Wild Bill and Quiet to give them some news.

"I looked on the Internet," Kendra said. "In a few months time, you won't be in the Wild West Hall of Shame."

"We won't?" asked Quiet.

"No. You'll be in the Wild West Hall of *Fame!*"

"Quiet will be there for making the loudest burp in the world," added Dad. "And Wild Bill will be crowned the champion hiccuper of all time."

"Cool Cactus!" the cowboys yelled.

"Even Rumbler will be in the Hall of Fame," added Dad.

"For making the loudest stomach noises in the world?" asked Wild Bill.

"No," replied Kendra. "For floating in the sky on a rubber horse longer than anyone else ever has . . . or ever will!"

Then from far up in the blue sky, Dad and Kendra thought that they heard a voice yelling, "Ye-haaaaa!"

About the Author

Bill Condon

When Bill Condon was not quite 10-years-old, he was helping to rescue a whale that was stranded on a beach. Suddenly the whale swallowed him and swam back to sea. It wasn't a killer whale . . . but it was a sneaky one!

With a little luck on his side, Bill was able to escape fairly quickly. But ever since that day, he has had a tendency to blubber.

About the Illustrator

Geoff Hocking

Geoff Hocking started illustrating books for children during the 1970s, when he and his wife, Christine, lived and worked in London.

Since then, he has illustrated dozens of books, written some, painted pictures, built a house of mud, spent too much money on foreign cars, and taught design and illustration to hundreds of people.

He and Christine have three children. One is a fashion designer, one is a graphic designer, and one is a preteen who does crazy drawings and worries about losing his hair.